A LITTLE SP⊙T OF ORGANIZATION

Written & Illustrated by Diane Alber

To my children, Ryan and Anna

This ORGANIZATION book belongs to:

_____

_____

_____

First, let's find some containers we can put things into. Then we can start sorting them into piles of: TOYS, GAMES, CARS, and BLOCKS!

After a birthday is a great time to DONATE TOYS! It gives you a chance to go through toys you have outgrown because you now are a year older!

Look how amazing this room looks!

See? EVERYTHING HAS A SPOT, AND
THERE IS A SPOT FOR EVERYTHING!

Did you know ORGANIZING actually grows your memory? It does this by training your brain to separate and categorize things!

This can be used in READING! You have to keep track of many things at once while reading, like characters and plots, events, and details. Let's look at some other ways you can be ORGANIZED!

Creating a ROUTINE will not only help you remember to do things (like clean you room), it also helps you grow your RESPONSIBILITY SPOT and CONFIDENCE SPOT!

You can use magnets instead of drawing spots in the boxes!

WRITING DOWN NOTES helps you remember things you might forget. Just be sure to put the notes where you see them easily.

Library Book

Valentine Cards

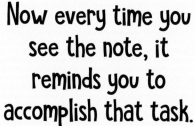

Cookies for Party

Now every time you see the note, it reminds you to accomplish that task.

March

SUNDAY	MONDAY	TUESDAY	WEDNESDAY	THURSDAY	FRIDAY	SATURDAY
1	2	3	4	5	6	7
8	9	10 Baseball	11 Dance	12	13	14 Baseball
15	16	17 St.Patty	18 Dance	19	20	21
22	23	24 Dance	25	26	27 National Scribble Day	28
29	30	31	1	2	3	4

-Anna 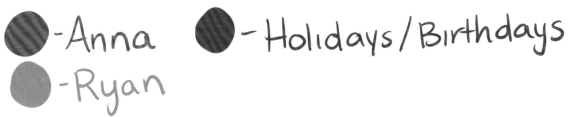-Holidays/Birthdays

-Ryan

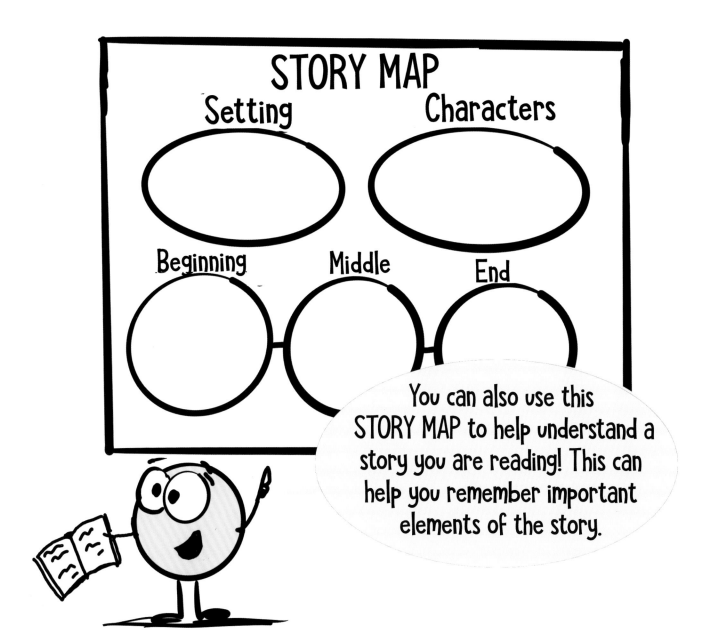

Oh, no! It looks like SCRIBBLE SPOT needs some help ORGANIZING his EMOTIONS!

If your EMOTIONS are feeling tangled,
ANXIETY, ANGER, or SADNESS
are probably nearby. The first step in organizing your
EMOTIONS is to identify what EMOTION you are
feeling so you can manage it!

LOOK! Scribble SPOT was able to identify what feeling he was having and guide it to his PEACEFUL SPOT!

Hopefully you were able to see how you can ORGANIZE some aspects of your life, from cleaning your room to managing your emotions.

I can't wait to see what you can ORGANIZE next!

"ORGANIZING WORKSHEETS" are FREE for download at www.dianealber.com